Friend Spider

written by
Jessica van Dessel

illustrated by
Diane Browning

PIONEER VALLEY EDUCATIONAL PRESS, INC.

"JACOB!"

I drop the milk pails and run. There's only one thing that can make my sweet Quaker mother scream like that.

She's standing by the barn door with her fingers pressed to her mouth. A huge spiderweb is stretched across the doorway. In the center sits a fat black spider. The spider is almost as big as my hand, with orange markings across its body. I've never seen one like it before.

"Oh, Jacob," she says, "get rid of that thing!"

"It's only a spider, Ma."

"Take it down!"

"But spiders are good creatures, Ma! They catch insects that do us harm!"

"Jacob, I am not going through that door until that thing is gone!"

I snap the threads of silk that hold the web to the doorframe. The spider scurries aside as the web breaks apart, waving its legs angrily.

I scoop up the floating threads until the web is gone. The spider hides in a hole on the doorframe. I don't have the heart to kill it, so I smack the wall, hoping this will chase it away and make Ma think it's been squashed.

"It's gone," I tell her. I go back to work. I've got lots to do. Pa left before dawn, heading for town to sell our four-year-old horses. While he's gone, I must take over his duties—including killing spiders for Ma.

I have finished most of my morning work when I see a man, woman, and two little girls coming through our wood lot. The man is John Freeman. He works for wages, not as the slave he was in Georgia before he ran away. I greet them cheerfully, but John is not smiling.

"Is your father here?" he asks. I shake my head.

"My husband will not be home until tomorrow night," says Ma, coming up behind me. "What is wrong?"

"Slave hunters, Missus Elton," says John.

Not long ago, the newspapers brought us news that slave owners could bring runaway slaves back to bondage. Reading this, Pa had said, "That will bring every good-for-nothing here to Ohio, looking for runaways to capture for a reward." It seems Pa was right.

"Can you hide us until dark?" John asks. "I don't want to bring trouble on your house, but there's no one else we can trust. I'm afraid they're not far behind."

Ma turns to me. "Where can we hide four people quickly?"

"The small hayloft over the horses' stall is empty," I say. John goes to take a look. The best we can do is to squeeze him and his family into a corner of the loft and pile barrels, boxes, and old rags around them. We stack tools and a broken wagon wheel in the stalls below. I hang a harness on the ladder too. It looks wrong, but perhaps a stranger will not notice.

"We must act as if nothing is different," Ma says as we return to the house. It's a good thing she is so calm. We've barely sat down to eat when we see riders coming up the lane.

I wish Pa was here. I want to run and hide, but I go out to stand beside Ma on the porch as four slave hunters ride up. Their leader doesn't get off his horse.

"You hiding any runaway slaves here, Ma'am?" he says. All you can see between his hat and beard is a purple nose.

"No," Ma replies. "There are no slaves here." I nearly laugh. My mother would never tell a lie. There are no slaves here, only John and his family, and they are free people.

"You won't mind, then," says the leader, "if we take a look." Two of his men are already going into our house. The leader and his partner ride slowly toward the barn. Before Ma can stop me, I follow them.

The men ignore me. They poke and kick everything, frightening our animals, spilling our oats. They search the big loft. I pray they will miss the smaller one, but no—the leader shoves the harness aside. He orders his partner to climb up. My heart is pounding in my ears. My fists are opening and closing. We Quakers are not supposed to fight, but right now I want to, even though I'm just a kid, even though I'm one against two.

Suddenly the man climbing the ladder stops. He is nose-to-nose with a huge spiderweb. The web stretches across the opening to the loft. In its center sits a very large, very hairy black-and-orange spider.

The man touches the web gingerly. The spider darts for his hand, and the man jumps clear off the ladder.

"Can't be anyone up there," he says.

"You sure?" asks the leader.

"Nothing's broken that web," says his partner. "See for yourself."

They look at the spider. It flexes its legs and works its mouth. "It must take days to spin a web that big," the leader says. "Nobody could've gotten past it today."

They throw a few more things around before giving up.

The other men come out of the house. Their leader bellows, "Anything?" The men shake their heads.

"I hope you are satisfied, gentlemen," says Ma. The men nod and hurry to leave.

Once they are out of sight, I grab Ma's arm and drag her to the barn. John is looking at the web.

"A miracle," he says.

Ma shudders. But then, slowly, a smile spreads across her face. "Yes. Jacob, I think we will leave Friend Spider in his home till nightfall."

The web protects John and his family until dark. Once the moon comes out, I show them the way to the river and see them off into the night. Canada is many miles away, but John says they have seen a miracle, and that means their journey will be successful.

Ma still doesn't much like spiders, but she doesn't ask me to kill them anymore. Sometimes I see her stop to gaze at a spiderweb when it's sparkling in the morning light.